WHAT IF TIGERS DISAPPEARED?

By Theresa Emminizer

Gareth Stevens
PUBLISHING

Please visit our website, www.garethstevens.com. For a free color catalog of all our high-quality books, call toll free 1-800-542-2595 or fax 1-877-542-2596.

Library of Congress Cataloging-in-Publication Data

Names: Emminizer, Theresa, author.
Title: What if tigers disappeared? / Theresa Emminizer.
Description: New York : Gareth Stevens, [2020] | Series: Life without animals
  | Includes index.
Identifiers: LCCN 2019006775| ISBN 9781538238301 (paperback) | ISBN
  9781538238325 (library bound) | ISBN 9781538238318 (6 pack)
Subjects: LCSH: Tiger–Conservation–Juvenile literature. | Endangered
  species–Juvenile literature.
Classification: LCC QL737.C23 E565 2020 | DDC 639.97/9756–dc23
LC record available at https://lccn.loc.gov/2019006775

Published in 2020 by
Gareth Stevens Publishing
111 East 14th Street, Suite 349
New York, NY 10003

Copyright © 2020 Gareth Stevens Publishing

Designer: Laura Bowen
Editor: Theresa Emminizer

Photo credits: cover, p. 1 MusiggachartSMY/Shutterstock.com; pp. 3-24 (series art) De-V/
Shutterstock.com; p. 5 Vinnie Lauritsen/Shutterstock.com; p. 7 (Bengal) neelsky/
Shutterstock.com; p. 7 (Sumatran) Sveta Imnadze/Shutterstock.com; p. 7 (Siberian) Jan Stria/
Shutterstock.com; p. 9 Ondrej Prosicky/Shutterstock.com; p. 11 (top) apiguide/Shutterstock.com;
p. 11 (bottom) Michal Ninger/Shutterstock.com; p. 13 Richard Constantinoff/Shutterstock.com;
p. 15 Saurin Munshaw/Shutterstock.com; p. 17 Andrew M. Allport/Shutterstock.com; p. 19
(bottom) Ammit Jack/Shutterstock.com; p. 19 Mickey-B/Wikimedia Commons; p. 21 Raj
Wildberry/Shutterstock.com.

Printed in the United States of America

CPSIA compliance information: Batch #CS19GS: For further information contact Gareth Stevens, New York, New York at 1-800-542-2595.

CONTENTS

Boldface words appear in the glossary.

Big Cats

Tigers are the biggest wild cats in the world! The largest weigh up to about 675 pounds (306 kg) and are nearly 10 feet (3 m) long. Tigers are top predators and affect all other **species** in their **ecosystems**. What would happen if they disappeared?

Tigers in Trouble

Today, tigers are **endangered**. There used to be nine subspecies, or different kinds, of tigers. Three of those subspecies have gone extinct, or died out completely, and one is extinct in the wild. There are less than 4,000 tigers in the wild.

Siberian tiger

Sumatran tiger

Bengal tiger

Where Do They Live?

Tigers once lived all across Asia. Now their **habitats** have become smaller and they live only in South and Southeast Asia, China, and the Russian Far East. Tigers live in all sorts of **environments**. Their habitats include forests, woodlands, grasslands, and more.

What Do They Eat?

Tigers are good swimmers, fast runners, and have powerful teeth and claws. They are meat eaters and hunt whatever they can catch, from goats to moose to crocodiles! They have been known to eat as much as 60 pounds (27 kg) of meat in a night.

Why Are They Important?

Other than humans, tigers have no predators. In their ecosystems, they are at the top of the food chain and affect all species within the habitat. They are important because they keep the population, or number, of **prey** species in check.

What Could Happen?

Many of the animals tigers hunt are plant eaters. In a way, by eating plant eaters, tigers **protect** the trees and other plants in their ecosystems. If tigers disappear, the populations of their prey species will rise. This prey could harm the ecosystems by eating too many plants.

15

If overeating caused plants to die out, the ecosystems could fail. Small animals and bugs that need plants could also disappear. The forests, woodlands, and grasslands where tigers once lived could turn into unlivable environments without any plants or animals.

What Harms Tigers?

Tigers are so important, but sadly they are not safe. People hunt tigers for their beautiful striped fur. Although hunting tigers is against the law, illegal hunters called poachers are still a **threat**. Tigers are also harmed by habitat loss.

tiger skin

19

You Can Help

The world needs tigers. Keeping them safe means keeping all the plants and animals in their ecosystems safe, too. You can help tigers by sharing what you've learned. Helping people better understand the importance of tigers will be a big part of protecting them.

GLOSSARY

ecosystem: all the living things in an area

endangered: in danger of dying out

environment: the natural world in which a plant or animal lives

habitat: the place or type of place where a plant or animal naturally lives and grows

prey: an animal that is hunted by other animals for food

protect: to keep safe

species: a group of plants or animals that are all of the same kind

threat: something likely to cause harm

FOR MORE INFORMATION

BOOKS

Clutton-Brock, Juliet. *Cat.* New York, NY: DK Children, 2014.

Simon, Seymour. *Big Cats.* New York, NY: HarperCollins Publishers, 2017.

WEBSITES

Defenders of Wildlife
defenders.org/tiger/basic-facts
Learn more fun facts about tigers.

World Wildlife Fund
worldwildlife.org/species/tiger
Find out how you can help tigers.

23

INDEX